How to Outplay a Bully

NOAH Hirji

How to Outplay a Bully

by

Nancy Wilcox Richards

illustrations by

David Sourwine

Scholastic Canada Ltd.

Toronto New York London Auckland Sydney
Mexico City New Delhi Hong Kong Buenos Aires

Scholastic Canada Ltd.
604 King Street West, Toronto, Ontario M5V 1E1, Canada

Scholastic Inc.
557 Broadway, New York, NY 10012, USA

Scholastic Australia Pty Limited
PO Box 579, Gosford, NSW 2250, Australia

Scholastic New Zealand Limited
Private Bag 94407, Botany, Manukau 2163, New Zealand

Scholastic Children's Books
Euston House, 24 Eversholt Street, London NW1 1DB, UK

Library and Archives Canada Cataloguing in Publication
Richards, Nancy Wilcox, 1958-
How to outplay a bully / Nancy Wilcox Richards ;
illustrations by David Sourwine.

ISBN 978-0-545-99738-6

1. Bullying — Juvenile fiction. I. Sourwine, David II. Title.

PS8585.I184H693 2008   jC813'.54   C2007-907498-7

ISBN-10 0-545-99738-0

6 5 4 3   Printed in Canada   116   12 13 14 15

For Jamie, who has retired from coaching
but is still crazy about the game,
and for all those cowbell-ringin', foghorn-blowin'
moms and dads who cheer on their kids.

— N. W. R.

The author would like to thank Bob MacMillan
for his assistance and support.

Chapter 1

My name is Tony —
Tony Dunphy. Tomorrow
I'm signing up to play
hockey with the Bayfield
Blazers. And I am pumped!
A lot of my friends are

already on the team. There's James and
Matthew and Nicholas. They've been Blazers
for a couple of years.

And Aaron begged me to join. "Please,
please, pleeeeeease. It's really fun. I know
you'll be great," he said, bouncing around.

So tomorrow is my first practice and I
can't wait.

My mom is really happy that I'm joining
the team, too. It wasn't always like that.

Playing hockey costs money. Lots of money. And that wasn't in her budget. But then last year this guy called Bobby bought the house next door. He saw our frozen pond out back and convinced my mom that it would be a perfect place for me to learn how to play. He would even teach me.

Bobby really loves skating and watching hockey on TV. Somehow he persuaded my mom to buy me some hockey gear. At first, Mom said no. Hockey gear is expensive. But he told her about the Kit Bag. It's a shop that sells second-hand stuff. Cheap. So along with skates, I finally have some gear. And tomorrow I get to skate with it on.

But first I have to get through today. Friday. The last day of school for the week. I have a spelling test, two pages of math to do and the best part of Grade Three — I have gym.

"And what do you think, Tony?" asked Ms MacArthur, my teacher.

I could tell by the smile on Ms

MacArthur's face that she knew I wasn't paying attention. And that's one of the reasons she's everybody's favourite teacher. Aside from no homework on the weekends and the jellybean machine that we get to use if we do our homework, Ms MacArthur never yells. Never. I've never even heard her raise her voice.

She repeated her question. "What do you think, Tony?"

"Uh . . ." I stammered, "um . . ." I felt my face get warm.

Ms MacArthur smiled and then she let me off the hook. "About ice safety." She looked directly at me before she continued. "Why would it be a good idea to carry a hockey stick when you're skating on a lake?"

I could feel everyone's eyes on me. Lauren, James, Matthew, Bethany, Nicholas.

"In case you fall through the ice," I answered. "You'd have a reaching assist."

Ms MacArthur nodded her head in agreement. Her eyes scanned the room. "Now, who can explain what a 'reaching assist' is?"

I slid lower in my seat. I felt a tap on my arm.

"Nice save," whispered Matthew. He's the goalie for the Bayfield Blazers. And he's always throwing in hockey terms whenever he can. "Bet I can guess what you were thinking about." Then he grinned at me.

I smiled back as Ms MacArthur walked away from my desk. I knew I could whisper a little without getting caught.

"I can't wait until tomorrow," I said out of the side of my mouth. "It's gonna be so much fun."

"Yeah, I know. We'll meet at the rink. Dressing Room 4."

"Okay," I answered, as Ms MacArthur stopped in front of my desk. She was looking down at me with the teacher look that says if you don't stop talking, you'll be in big trouble. So I put on my best I-am-really-paying-attention face and tried to listen as she talked about ice safety. But all I could think about was hockey. My very first practice was tomorrow. I finally had hockey gear. I was going to be a Bayfield Blazer. And even though I was joining the team halfway through the season, I knew it was going to be awesome.

Chapter 2

I got up really early on Saturday morning. By six o'clock I had my hockey bag packed. Then unpacked. Then packed again. I wanted to be certain I had everything I needed. I even made sure that my water bottle was filled. By seven o'clock I was sitting at the kitchen table staring at the clock.

Finally Mom walked into the kitchen, yawning. She looked at me with sleepy eyes and yawned again. "You're up early, Tony."

"Today's the big day, Mom."

"I know." She smiled. She poured coffee into her favourite blue mug. "Bayfield Blazers, here you come!"

"Can we go now?" I begged. "Pleeeease."

Mom laughed. "Could I have my coffee first? Maybe grab a shower and get dressed before we head out?"

"How long will that take?" I asked. "Can you be fast?"

Mom sighed. "Eat some cereal. Give me twenty minutes." She took a long swallow of coffee. As she headed down the hall, I could hear her muttering something about "needing her beauty rest."

The first thing I noticed when we walked through the rink doors, besides the butterflies in my stomach, was the smell. Cold and damp, like Grandpa's basement.

Mom pointed to the other end of the rink. "I think the dressing rooms are down that way," she said.

I nodded and swallowed.

"I'll be back at the end of practice," she said. Her eyebrows were scrunched together.

"Are you sure you don't need any help getting your skates laced?"

"Yup," I answered. "See you later."

Dressing Room 4 was crowded. Kids sat on the benches lined against the wall. Some of them already had their gear on. Matthew waved to me. "Hey, Tony!" he shouted. "I saved you a spot." He patted the empty space on the bench next to him.

I looked around the room. Some of the kids, like James and Aaron, I knew. Some I didn't.

I started pulling my gear out of the bag. "Who's that?" I whispered to Matthew, nodding in the direction of two big kids sitting across the room.

Matthew glanced over and lowered his voice, "That's Berk. And Drew. They're . . ."

But before he had chance to finish, one of the boys pointed at Matthew and snarled, "Who are you looking at?"

A few kids looked at Matthew. Then they looked back at the big kid.

"I said," and Big Kid raised his voice, "who are you looking at?"

"No one, Berk," came Matthew's quick reply. "I'm just telling Tony who some of the kids on the team are." And he started fiddling with his shin pad.

I took a quick peek at Berk, just in time to see him elbow his friend. Then he pointed at me and said something I couldn't hear. But I could tell he was talking about me. He was pointing and laughing.

I looked down at my gear. Maybe I put something on backwards. Nope. Everything was looking good. In fact, everything was looking great. The shoulder pads were sturdy. The elbow pads fit perfectly.

Matthew whispered out of the side of his mouth, "They're both mean and . . ."

Laughter interrupted him. Berk and Drew were jabbing each other in the ribs. Berk pointed at me and then he said in a loud voice so that everyone could hear, "*Eeew*. Check out Tony's gear!"

The dressing room fell silent. Everyone stared at me. Then suddenly all the kids got very busy. Lacing skates. Taping sticks. Digging into hockey bags.

I glanced down at my new-to-me gear.

"Where'd you dig that up? The garbage can?" Berk sneered at me.

"Probably at a second-hand store," chimed in Drew.

"Looooooser," Berk said in a slow drawl.

"Looooooser," echoed Drew.

I looked at Drew. Then at Berk. I knew my gear wasn't top-of-the-line like theirs. I knew it wasn't brand new. But it was still good gear and it was all my mom could afford. I wanted to say, "I know who the loser is. It's you, Berk. And your buddy, Drew." But the words just wouldn't come out. Instead, I reached into my bag, pretending to look for my gloves. And the dressing room was quiet. Really quiet.

Chapter 3

The team headed for the ice, with Matthew and me at the back of the line. I took a deep breath. This was it. Finally, a chance to play hockey. All my skating on the pond with Bobby was finally going to pay off. I just knew it. I smiled at Matthew. He smiled back with a look that said, You okay? before he joined the others on the ice.

Everyone was warming up and getting ready to do drills. For a minute I watched them skate around. Then I stepped out onto the ice. This was going to be so much fun!

Crash! One minute I was stepping onto the ice and the next I was doing a nose plant. I stole a quick look at Berk and Drew. Sure enough they were staring straight at me, big grins on their faces. What happened? Skating on a pond wasn't that different from a rink, was it?

"Hey, Tony," Aaron said, leaning down close to my face. "You forgot to take off your skate guards."

I glanced down and groaned. How could I be so dumb? "Thanks," I mumbled to Aaron, but not before I heard Berk holler from the other side of the rink.

"Hey, Tony! Tony Baloney! Can't you even skate?"

So now I was Tony Baloney. Great. Just great.

I yanked off my skate guards and tossed them over the boards. I'd pick them up at the end of practice. Then I circled around the rink, watching what the other kids on the team were doing. The skating part wasn't so bad — now that I wasn't wearing guards. But some of the stretches were tough. My helmet felt heavy and the gear was awkward. Aaron zipped by me. Quickly he reversed, skating by me backward this time. "So, what do you think?" he asked. "Isn't this fun? Just wait till we scrimmage!"

I smiled back. "It's starting to get better," I agreed. I turned to skate backward just like Aaron did. Except with all that gear, it was tricky. One second I was turning. The next second I was sprawled flat on my butt. My stick went shooting across the ice and hit the boards. I couldn't believe it. I never have trouble switching direction. It had to be the gear. I just wasn't used to it. Before I could get up, some kid with number 58 on his jersey was skating backward toward me, and he was picking up speed. He hadn't seen me go down. *Crash!* He landed right on my chest. Then James fell on him. And Ozzie on top of him. And then Ahmed.

I was squashed like a bug under all those guys. I couldn't breathe. It felt like an elephant was sitting on me. It seemed like forever until everyone got off. I took a deep breath. The cold air felt good. Then

something caught my eye. I turned toward centre ice. There stood Berk and Drew, pointing at me. And they were laughing. Again.

"Hey, Tony! Tony Baloney! That's some skating!" Berk yelled. His voice echoed. He turned round and round on his skates and waved his arms in the air. "Oh, oh, oh!" he cried in a high, fake voice. "I can't skate. I'm falling." And then he threw himself down on the ice. He was laughing so hard, he started to cough. Drew looked over at me. Then he looked down at Berk and said something. The two of them laughed really loud. And I knew they were laughing at me. I hung my head.

"Come on, Tony," encouraged James. "Coach is waiting for us down by the net." Then he lowered his voice. "Don't let them get to you."

I nodded and skated over to join the rest of the Blazers. When Berk and Drew joined us, they were still laughing — hard enough that Berk started coughing.

The coach looked over. "Take a breather, Berk. Go sit on the bench until you get that coughing under control."

Berk skated toward the bench, hacking the whole way.

Chapter 4

When we got back to the dressing room, I took a long drink from my water bottle. I was hot and sweaty. My hair was plastered to my head.

"That was fun," I told Aaron. I stole a quick peek at Drew and Berk. "At least most of it was fun."

Aaron smiled back. "I knew you'd make a great Blazer."

Just then the coach interrupted our conversation. "Good practice today, boys. Most of you worked really hard. Now, I have just one reminder." He looked around the room to make sure he had everyone's attention. The room was quiet. Coach cleared his throat. He wrote something on

his clipboard using a large black marker. "What does this say?" he asked, as he held the clipboard up for everyone to see. "Berk?"

Berk squirmed on the bench. "'Team,' Coach. It says 'team.'"

"That's right. And how do we spell it?" He was still looking at Berk.

"T–E–A–M," Berk answered, sounding confused. "Anybody can see that."

There was a pause before Coach went on. "Yes, Berk, anyone can see that 'team' is spelled T–E–A–M." Then he turned to face the rest of the Blazers.

"There is no 'I' in 'team.' That means we all pull together. We pass the puck." He paused and looked directly at Berk. "No one can win this game alone. But together, the Blazers can be . . . No," he corrected himself, "the Blazers are an awesome team. But we have to work as . . . " he paused.

" . . . a *team*!" everyone yelled.

Coach smiled. "Exactly. Now, I'll see all of you on Tuesday after school."

I took another long drink from my water bottle. I looked over at Berk. He had this mad look on his face. He was throwing his gear into his hockey bag. He stopped and glared at me. "What are you staring at, Tony Baloney?"

"N-n-nothing," I stammered. I bent over and began to unlace my skates.

Chapter 5

On Monday during math class, I was still thinking about being a Bayfield Blazer. And even though it wasn't easy skating with a ton of gear on, I knew I'd get used to it. The practice had been great. Not perfect, because of Berk and Drew. But almost perfect. I was just picturing scoring my first goal when Ms MacArthur interrupted my thoughts. "Time to put away our math books, class. We'll play a round of Stump the Expert."

The class cheered. This is everyone's favourite game. Teams score points for correct answers. At the end of the month, the team with the most points wins cafeteria coupons. Then you get to pick whatever treat you want. Our cafeteria is trying out all these healthy new food choices. And I know that winning the coupons is just another way to get kids to stop eating junk food. But I don't care. It's free food.

"Now for our first question," said Ms MacArthur. "It's from the History category. What famous fishing schooner is on the Canadian dime?"

Right away Lauren waved her arm back and forth.

"Lauren?" asked Ms MacArthur.

"The *Bluenose!*"

"You're right," answered Ms MacArthur. "That's one point for Lauren's table." Ms MacArthur scored a point on the board. "Question number two," she continued, "is from the Literature category. Who is the famous redhead from Prince Edward Island?" She looked around the room.

Matthew slowly raised his hand.

"Who do you think, Matthew?"

"Clifford the Big Red Dog?"

Ms MacArthur smiled. "That's a good try, but no. That's not the right answer. Does anyone else have a guess?" She waited. Then she repeated the question. "Who is the famous redhead from Prince Edward Island?" When no one else answered, she said, "It's Anne of Green Gables."

Bethany groaned. "I should have known that. I saw the play in Charlottetown last summer."

"Here's our last question for the day." Ms MacArthur paused. "It's from the Sports category. Before the 1917-1918 season, what *weren't* goalies allowed to do?"

Quickly I raised my hand. "I know this!" I whispered to Aaron and Matthew at my table. "My neighbour Bobby tells me lots of neat hockey stuff. He knows everything about hockey!"

"Tony, before the 1917-1918 season what weren't goalies allowed to do?" repeated Ms MacArthur.

"I'm pretty sure they weren't allowed to

fall on the ice to make a save," I answered.

"You are absolutely right. That's a point for your table, Tony." Ms MacArthur looked around the room. "So, boys and girls, that wraps up another round of Stump the Expert for today. Now, it's time for recess. Remember your hats and zip up those jackets. It's really cold today."

I sat next to Aaron and Lauren on the bench outside our classroom, tugging on my boots.

"Looks like we might win Stump the Expert for January," said Aaron. "We're ahead by two points." And he high-fived me.

I smiled back. "That was an easy question." I paused. "But it's not going to be easy to get Berk to stop calling me names. He's going to call me Tony Baloney forever."

"He's such a bully," agreed Aaron.

"And Berk's not that great a player. He could barely skate from one end of the rink to the other without coughing or taking a break," I complained.

Aaron pulled on his mittens and looked right at me. "He's got asthma, I think. Sometimes I see him use a puffer."

"Oh," I said. Now it all made sense. The coughing and wheezing. But that didn't change anything. He was still mean. He was still a bully.

I could tell that Lauren was listening to our conversation. She had stopped zipping her jacket and was looking at the two of us. "I had troubles with a bully." She lowered her voice and pointed down the hall at a girl in a striped hat. "Bethany. And it was definitely not fun."

Playing for the Bayfield Blazers was going to be fun. Tons of fun. But dealing with Berk was not going to be any fun at all. I was going to be Tony Baloney for a long time. Probably for the rest of my life.

Chapter 6

School seemed to last forever on Tuesday. Ms MacArthur was out sick. That meant we had a substitute teacher. And that meant no Stump the Expert. It felt like the hands on the clock were stuck, but they weren't. I could actually hear it ticking, because when Mrs. Grant teaches us, there is no talking. And I mean none. We're not even allowed to whisper. Finally the bell rang. Now the best part of the day would start. Hockey practice.

When I got to the rink, kids were already in the dressing room changing.

"Hey, Tony! Sit here!" hollered Matthew.

He looked huge wearing all his goalie gear. Almost like he should be in junior high school.

I sat down and looked around the room. Right away I saw Berk and Drew. I swallowed hard. I could feel my heart beating in my chest. I scanned the rest of the room. Aaron was there. And Nicholas. And James. "Where's the coach?" I asked.

"He had to make a phone call," answered Matthew. "He'll be right back. Why?"

I eyed Berk and Drew again. My heart started to speed up. "No reason. I was just wondering."

Getting dressed was easier and faster this time. And the gear didn't feel as weird. I knew skating wouldn't be a problem today. I glanced down at my skates. This time I remembered to take off my skate guards. I was all set.

"Okay Blazers! Let's go!" came a voice from across the room.

I knew without looking that the voice

belonged to Berk. The team all headed in his direction. Slowly I stood up and walked toward the group.

Berk watched me. He waited until I was halfway across the room before he said, "Not *you*, Tony Baloney. We want real Blazers. Guys who can skate. That sure isn't you."

I stopped. The room grew quiet. Some of the kids looked at me and then back to Berk. Most of the kids looked at the floor.

"Sit down, Tony Baloney," he ordered.

I gulped. I looked around the room. No one looked back at me. And I knew why. Everyone was afraid of Berk.

"Yeah, Tony Baloney. He said to sit down," snarled Drew.

I wondered if he meant right here. Sit on the floor. Or was I allowed to go back to the bench? I swallowed hard. And sat right on the floor.

"Look at that," laughed Berk. "Tony Baloney isn't even smart enough to sit on the bench."

"Lay off of him," said Matthew.

Berk looked at Matthew. "Who's gonna make me? *You*?" He took a menacing step toward him.

Matthew glanced sympathetically at me. I knew he'd tried his best to help me.

"Okay, Blazers," continued Berk. "Ready?"

I watched as they all extended their arms. And then Berk chanted, "Bayfield Blazers are so cool. Bayfield Blazers really rule!"

Then all the kids tapped knuckles. "Go, Blazers!" chanted the whole team. One by one the team left the dressing room and headed out toward the ice. I got up off the dressing-room floor. "I will not let Berk get to me," I silently repeated in my head. "I will not let Berk get to me."

Chapter 7

Once I was on the ice, I knew I was right. The skating was easier. My hockey gear felt better.

Aaron skated over to me. "You're getting better, Tony." He grinned at me. "I see you remembered to take off your skate guards today."

"Yeah, that was kind of dumb." I grinned back. "I did some extra practising on the pond behind our house on the weekend. Bobby gave me a few more tips. I think it's working." I turned to skate backwards. And this time I didn't fall. Not even close. "Race you to the blue line!"

Ozzie, Ahmed and I took turns taking shots on Matthew. He made some awesome saves. Then Coach called us over to the centre line.

"Okay, guys," he began, "we're going to begin the practice with a few skating drills. Everyone will start at the goal line. Skate your fastest to the blue line and do a two-foot stop. Then back to the goal line." He looked at all of us. He pointed to centre ice. "The next time, you race to the centre line. Do a two-foot stop. And back to the goal line. Any questions?" When no one said anything, he continued. "Advance one line at a time until you're skating from one goal line to the other." He paused and pulled a stopwatch out of his pocket. "I'm going to time you. Now, everyone on the goal line."

I lined up next to Aaron and Ozzie.

"Ready, set . . . go!" yelled the coach.

I raced for the blue line, made a quick stop, and turned back for the goal line. A quick turn and I was headed back for centre ice. Aaron was a bit ahead of me but not by much. Ozzie was right behind me. Out of the corner of my eye I noticed Berk, trailing way behind. His face was pale and he was breathing really hard. I made a quick two-foot stop at centre, pushing down hard on my skates. It sounded like they were eating into the ice. I tore off for the goal line again. That's when I noticed Berk had stopped skating. He was bent over taking big gulps of air. He was wheezing really badly. It sounded like he couldn't breathe. I skated over to him.

"You all right?" I asked.

Berk stared at me angrily.

"Duh," he said. Then he shoved me. Hard. I lost my balance and started to fall, but at the last second I caught myself. Berk pushed past me. His wheezing was even worse. He skated over to the boards, kicked open the players' door with his skate, and stormed off to the dressing room.

What a jerk, I thought.

I didn't realize how wiped I was from the skating until I was back in the dressing room. My legs felt like rubber. My face was covered in sweat. And I was thirsty — really thirsty. I reached for my water bottle. It was empty. I held it up to the light and gave it a shake. Yup. Empty all right. But how could that be?

I stuck it in my hockey bag. That's when I noticed more trouble. All of my clothes seemed to be wet. I pulled out my T-shirt. Soggy. I pulled out my sweater. Soaked. Even my pants were dripping. What was going on?

That's when I discovered my third problem. My boots. They were filled with snow. Right to the top. And then I knew. Berk! He had left the ice early. He had had all kinds of time to empty my water bottle over my clothes. He had even had enough time to fill my boots with snow.

I stared at him. He was already changed and sitting next to Drew, waiting for him to get out of his hockey gear. He took a long

slow drink from his water bottle and looked straight at me. Then he stopped drinking and gave his bottle a little tap. All the time, he was looking right at me. And then he said in a loud voice, "All that skating sure does make me thirsty." And he laughed. "Does it make you thirsty, Drew?"

"Sure does," agreed Drew and he stopped unlacing his skates and looked over at me. "Sure does." Then both he and Berk laughed.

Chapter 8

The next day at school I tried to forget about my snow-filled boots. And my soaked clothes. And Berk shoving me. It was a good thing Ms MacArthur was back to play Stump the Expert, because I like that game so much that I can forget about almost anything. And that includes my troubles with Berk and all his bullying.

Ms MacArthur waited for the class to be quiet before she asked the first question. She cleared her throat. It was like a signal. Finally Matthew got the hint and stopped talking to James.

"So," Ms MacArthur said, "we're ready to start." She looked at Matthew first and then James. "Our first question today is from the

Sports category."

I leaned forward a bit, waiting for the question. This was my favourite category.

"What were some of the first hockey pucks made of?"

Claire's hand shot into the air. "Was it rubber?" she asked.

Ms MacArthur shook her head. "No, sorry, Claire. It wasn't rubber. Does anyone else have a guess?" She looked around the room.

I tried to remember if Bobby ever talked about hockey pucks. But I couldn't remember him saying anything.

"Believe it or not," Ms MacArthur said, "some of the first hockey pucks were made of frozen horse dung."

Some of the class groaned.

"Dung?" asked Ahmed. "What's that?"

I heard a few kids snicker and before Ms MacArthur could answer, someone shouted from the back of the room, "Poop! The first puck was made of horse poop!"

"*Eeew*, gross," muttered Claire. "I liked my answer better."

"Now for question number two," continued Ms MacArthur. "This is a true or false Science question. The aardvark, also known as an anteater, has the largest tongue in the world." Ms MacArthur held up a drawing of a large grey anteater. She nodded at Bethany who was jumping up and down next to her seat.

"I know, I know!" yelled Bethany. "That answer is false!"

Ms MacArthur smiled. "You're right, Bethany. The blue whale has the largest tongue in the world. It weighs more than an elephant. In fact, fifty people could stand on its tongue. That's a point for your table." She added Bethany's point to the board.

Bethany turned and faced me, doing a victory dance. Then she stuck out her tongue at me, but it was pretty small compared to the blue whale's. "We're just two points behind you, Tony," she boasted.

I laughed. "We'll still win. Just wait and see."

"Here is our last question for the day," interrupted Ms MacArthur. "It's from the Nature category. What three things *won't* you find in Newfoundland?"

Nature . . . So the three things had to be plants or animals. But what could they be? "Any ideas?" I whispered to Aaron and Matthew. They shook their heads.

"I don't think there are any skunks in Newfoundland, but I'm not sure what the others are," I said.

Whispers filled the room but no one had an answer.

"Anyone want to give it a try?"

Slowly Aaron raised his hand. "I think the answer might be skunks, snakes and . . . "

Ms MacArthur waited for him to finish. "You need to name one more thing, Aaron." She paused. "What is the last living thing?"

"Is it sunflowers?" he asked.

Ms MacArthur shook her head. "You were so close," she answered. "The three things you won't find in Newfoundland are skunks, snakes and poison ivy. That was a good attempt, Aaron."

"Nice try," I whispered. "But we're still ahead by two points."

After Stump the Expert we lined up for lunch. I could smell the pepperoni pizza as soon as I walked into the cafeteria. I wondered what my mom had packed. My stomach made a gurgling noise. I grabbed the last seat by the window. It was next to James. I eyed his tuna sandwich with carrot sticks on the side.

"That looks good," I said, as I opened my lunch box.

James bit into a carrot. "What have you got?"

I started to unpack my lunch. I had apple juice, a container of chocolate pudding, a box of raisins and some kind of sandwich wrapped in foil. I smelled it and scrunched my face. "Yuck, it's egg. Smell." And I shoved the sandwich under James' nose.

"Gross. Smells rotten," he said.

"Egg sandwiches always smell that way," I said. "Like horse dung. Maybe I should freeze it and use it for a puck."

James laughed. We sat eating quietly for a few minutes and then he turned toward me. He had this look that he gets when he's thinking about something serious.

"That Berk is being so mean," he said. "Maybe you should let him know how it feels. Hide his hockey stick so he can't play."

"Yeah," I agreed. "Or put glue in his mouthguard." I laughed, warming up to the idea. "That would be funny. I can just see his face."

"I know what!" James said excitedly. "You know how our names are sewn on the back of our jerseys?"

I nodded.

"Well, take a marker and change the B to a J," laughed James. "Instead of Berk he'll be Jerk."

I laughed back. "That would be perfect! Because that's what he is — a jerk." And I high-fived James.

Then he got that serious look on his face again. "It probably wouldn't work, though."

I slumped in my seat. "You're right. But it's sure fun thinking up stuff."

James was quiet for a moment. "Yeah. But you can't let him know he's getting to you."

Chapter 9

Saturday finally arrived — the day of my first official game. I was really pumped about playing the Malone Mariners, and maybe just a bit nervous at the same time.

When I walked into Dressing Room 4 most of the team was already there. I dropped my bag next to Ozzie's and started putting on my gear. Shin pads, elbow pads, shoulder pads. I was just reaching for my skates when the door opened. In strolled Berk and Drew.

Berk took a long look at me.

"Hey, Tony Baloney!" he called out. "Coach wants to see you."

"Now?" I asked.

Berk looked back at Drew. He nodded his

head and smiled. "Yup, right now. And he said to hurry."

"He's down by the main entrance," added Drew.

I looked at Ozzie. He shrugged his shoulders.

"I'll be right back," I told Ozzie.

I left the dressing room and quickly hurried down the long corridor. I was thinking that maybe Coach wanted to put me on the starting line. Maybe he was going to let me play centre instead of right wing. That would be so cool.

I picked up speed as I got closer to the entrance. I scanned the doorway. Spectators were already starting to arrive. I spied Lauren and Claire coming in with their dads but there was no sign of Coach. Where was he? Maybe he was at the side entrance. I made a quick left turn and headed for the other doors. The entrance was empty. Now what do I do? I stood there, thinking. I didn't know where else to look.

"Hi, Tony," said a voice from behind.

I turned. I was surprised to see Ms MacArthur. "Oh, hi, Ms MacArthur. What are you doing here?"

She smiled down at me. "I'm here to cheer on my favourite team. Are you playing today?" She looked at her watch. "I think the game starts in just a few minutes. Shouldn't you be out on the ice?"

Oh no! The game! I was going to be late. "Have you seen Coach?" I blurted out. "I'm supposed to find him."

Ms MacArthur shook her head. "Sorry. I just got here."

"Well, thanks anyway. I gotta go." I turned and raced back to the dressing room.

I could hear Ms MacArthur's voice echoing down the hallway, "Good luck, Tony!"

When I finally got back to the dressing room, it was empty. The team was already on the ice. It was a good thing I was already dressed. The only thing I had to do was put on my skates. I dug through my bag. My hand searched one end, then the other. No skates. That's weird. They have to be here. Frantically I pawed through the bag. Nothing! "I know I packed them," I muttered. "I know I packed them." But where were they?

And then, like you see in the cartoons, a light came on. I knew the coach had never

wanted to see me. Berk had just said that. He set me up! He was trying to stop me from playing my first game.

I took a deep breath. My skates had to be someplace. But where? I picked up jackets and pants. I looked under benches. No skates. Then I got an awful feeling in the pit of my stomach. I headed toward the washroom. Not even Berk could be that mean. Or could he?

There are three toilets in the washroom. I lifted the lid on the first one. I was afraid to look. Nothing. I lifted the lid on the second one. Nothing. Slowly I walked over to the last toilet. If my skates were in there, I knew they would be ruined. My hockey days would be over before they even got started. I couldn't bear to look. I crossed my fingers and lifted the lid.

Chapter 10

There was — nothing. Absolutely nothing. What a relief. But I still had a major problem. Where were my skates? I knew I had packed them.

I turned in a circle, thinking. From the mirror over the sinks, the blue and silver crest that spelled Bayfield Blazers sparkled back at me. Some Blazer I turned out to be. I couldn't even find my own skates. I straightened my jersey. That's when I noticed another reflection. Something silver in the garbage can ... I ran over and threw a pile of soggy paper towels onto the floor. My hand hit something hard and leathery. There were my skates! I felt like jumping up and down. But my team needed me. Now.

It seemed to take forever to lace up my skates. The more I tried to hurry, the more I fumbled. I was never going to get out on the ice. And it was all Berk's fault.

My eyes began to water. Angrily I brushed away the tears. That's when I remembered what James had said. *You can't let him know he's getting to you.*

I gave a quick yank on my laces, stood up and straightened my jersey. I won't, I thought. I headed out to join the team.

I slid onto the end of the bench next to Ahmed. Coach was pacing back and forth behind the team, watching the game and chewing rapidly on a piece of gum. Then he narrowed his eyes at me and frowned. "You're late, Tony," he barked. "The game started three minutes ago." He pointed to the clock at the far end of the ice.

I gulped. So much for a great start to my first game. I stole a glance at Berk. He was sitting at the other end with Drew. The two of them were smirking at me. It was like they were getting a kick out of Coach being mad at me. I wanted to shout out what they'd done to make me late.

But James' words echoed in my head. *You can't let him know he's getting to you.*

I sat a little straighter on the bench and I looked Coach right in the eye. "Sorry, Coach," I said. "It won't happen again."

Then I looked over at Berk. He was still watching me. But now he didn't have a smirk on his face. Now he looked . . . surprised.

Chapter 11

A few minutes later Coach tapped me on the shoulder. "Okay, Tony." He smiled at me. "Let's go. You play right wing. Berk will play centre." Finally it was my turn on the ice. I stepped onto the ice with Berk. "And remember boys, pass that puck! This is a team sport."

The Malone Mariners were ahead 2–1. It was still anybody's game. I wondered if maybe I'd score my first goal today. That would be sweet. The referee blew the whistle and the puck was dropped.

The teams were pretty evenly matched. I felt good. I could easily keep up with the other players. But it only took one shift on the ice for me to realize something. Every

Blazer was doing exactly what the coach said: passing the puck, working together. Everybody that is, except Berk. Surprise, surprise. Every time he got the puck, he tried to score a goal all by himself.

"Pass the puck!" James yelled. He was in a perfect position to score. But did Berk pass the puck? No. And to make matters worse, he started to cough and wheeze. His skating slowed down. I saw Coach signal him to come off the ice. I was pretty sure that Berk saw him, too, but he continued to try to score a goal all by himself. It was like James and I didn't even exist.

After that, every shift was the same. Whenever Berk got the puck, he refused to pass. The score was still 2–1. If only we could score. Then came my big chance. The Malone Mariners goalie was actually behind his net. It was wide open — the perfect opportunity to score and tie the game. "Pass it here, Berk!" I hollered, banging my stick on the ice.

Berk looked at me. He saw that I was in front of the net. He hesitated.

I heard Coach holler from the bench, "Pass the puck! Pass it!"

I banged my stick on the ice again. "I'm open, Berk. Pass!" In disbelief, I watched as he tried to skate through two Mariners. There was no way he could get by them. He was struggling, and they were huge. And fast.

Berk was knocked to the ice. Number 15

of the Mariners stole the puck and started skating in the opposite direction. He had a breakaway! He wound up for the slapshot. It sailed past Matthew's open glove into the top right-hand corner of the net. Goal!

I hung my head and skated off the ice. We were now trailing 3–1 and all because of Berk.

I sat down on the bench next to him. He didn't even look at me. But I was so mad I had to say something.

"Why didn't you pass the puck?" I yelled. "I could have scored! I was right in front of the open net." I knew I shouldn't say any more but it was like I couldn't help it. All those feelings I had kept inside were bubbling out. "You're not a team player! You're a puck·hog!"

"Tony!" Coach's tone was sharp. "No name-calling on this team, no matter how frustrating it gets out there. Understand?"

I nodded. No one on the bench said a word.

Chapter 12

January zoomed by and before I knew it, it was February. The best days were always Tuesdays and Saturdays. Those were the days I had hockey practice or a game.

Berk was still being a pain. But I was trying not to let him get to me, even when he called me Tony Baloney. Sometimes he'd jeer at me, saying stuff like, "Anybody see a hog around here?" Then he'd snort like a pig. I knew he was thinking back to the day we lost to the Malone Mariners, the day I called him a puck hog. I tried my best to ignore him, but it was hard. Really hard.

We were just finishing a passing drill. It was my turn to shoot the puck to Berk, when I heard him start to snort like a pig. *Snort, snort.* "Here, puck hog!" he called. "Here hoggy-hog!" I could see Drew snickering near the blue line.

Why was Berk calling me a puck hog? He should take a look in the mirror. But I didn't have time to think too much about it because Coach's voice boomed across the ice, "That's enough, Berk! We work as a team. None of this foolishness. Got it?"

Berk's face turned red.

"Now, you two boys work on passing that puck smoothly to each other."

And that's what we did. We passed the puck back and forth, back and forth. Silently.

Coach blew his whistle and signalled for the team to meet at centre ice. "We're going to finish today's practice with a speed-skating drill. We'll form two teams and race each other around the pylons while stickhandling the puck. Let's go!" He clapped his hands together.

I got in line behind Ahmed and James. The coach blew his whistle and I watched as Aaron and Drew raced each other around the pylons. They were pretty evenly matched and Drew won by just a few seconds. A few more pairs raced. Then it was my turn — and wouldn't you know it? I had to race against Berk. Talk about bad luck.

Coach blew his whistle. I pushed off with

my right skate, the blade digging into the ice. I kept my two hands on the stick, making sure the puck wasn't too far ahead of me. Berk had a head start, but not by much. I was pretty sure I could catch him. And then he started to cough. I was gaining on him. I skated around one pylon, then another. I passed him. Even though he was still coughing, he managed to give me the evil eye. He was ticked. I raced for the last pylon. I won!

I watched as Berk skated around the last two pylons. I couldn't tell if his face was red from wheezing and coughing or he was just that mad.

"I could have won," he wheezed. "I'm a lot faster than you." He paused, trying to catch his breath. "It's just . . . "

But I didn't stick around to hear what else he had to say. I skated past him and headed for the other end of the rink. Berk turned, following me. We were just about at

centre ice when I felt a push from behind and I went crashing into the bin of spare pylons. They went flying in every direction and I landed with a thud among them.

Berk skated past me. "Sorry, Tony Baloney." He grinned down at me. "I tripped."

I glared at him. But before I could say anything, I heard Coach holler, "Pick up those pylons, Tony. Practice is just about over!"

So I spent the last few minutes of practice picking up thirteen orange pylons. Every time I tossed one into the bin, I pretended it was Berk, landing with a thump at the bottom. Somehow it made me feel better.

Chapter 13

After I finished picking up the pylons, I headed for the dressing room. Most of the kids were getting changed. I plopped down next to Matthew. I unsnapped my helmet and dropped it into my bag. Then I grabbed my water bottle and took a long drink. The cold water felt good.

"Good practice today, Tony," said Matthew.

"Yeah, except for how it ended."

Matthew nodded sympathetically.

I glanced over at Berk. He didn't look different from any other kid on the team. You'd never know by looking at him that he was such a bully. But he was. I sighed and reached down to untie my skates.

Once I was changed, I started to arrange my gear in my hockey bag. I wanted to be sure that I didn't leave anything behind. There was nothing on the bench or under the bench. I took one last quick look around to be certain I had everything. That's when I noticed Berk. He was still sitting there in his hockey gear. It was like he was being a slowpoke on purpose.

By now, half the kids on the team had left.

"See you next practice!" hollered Aaron.

"Bye!" yelled Matthew.

I waved as they headed out the door. I saw Berk take a quick glance around the dressing room. Then slowly he began to peel off his gear, starting with his jersey, then his elbow and shoulder pads. He paused and took another look around. He caught me watching him. He hesitated for a minute. Then he took off the last of his hockey gear.

I couldn't believe what I saw. There stood the meanest kid on the Bayfield Blazer

hockey team in teddy bear long johns. Yup. They were covered in cute little blue and green teddy bears!

My eyes went to his face — his very red face. Berk was staring intently back at me.

I thought about all the mean things he had done: calling me Tony Baloney, making fun of my second-hand gear, filling my boots with snow, shutting me out of the Blazer chant, knocking me into the pylons. Now was my chance to get even. Some tough guy he turned out to be. I looked around the room. No one else had noticed the teddy bears. They were all too busy yakking and packing up.

I shook my head. I didn't say a word.

A look of relief washed over his face. Then he quickly finished getting dressed.

Chapter 14

Before I knew it, it was March. The team was busy suiting up for the last practice of the season when Coach said he had an important announcement to make. Everyone stopped. All eyes were focused on him.

"Well, boys," he began, "our hockey season is winding down. We've come a long way since our first practice in the fall. There have been some nice improvements with the team." Coach scanned the room, looking at every Bayfield Blazer. "Our skating has gotten better. Our shooting is stronger and more accurate. Some of us still need a bit more work in the sportsmanship department." He paused and looked directly at Drew and Berk. Then he cleared his throat. "But, all in all, I am happy with how this team has pulled together."

I looked around the room. Some of the kids were nodding their heads. Others were smiling.

"So — I have arranged for a treat to end our season," Coach continued. "We are going to have a special guest come to our last game." He paused again. "Our mystery guest is a real hockey pro from the NHL."

Everyone started yelling and cheering.

"Cool!" yelled James. "Who is it?"

You know someone from the NHL?" asked Aaron.

Coach nodded. "Now, I'll let you boys try to figure out who our special guest might be, but I will give you this hint." He paused, making sure he had our attention. When there wasn't a sound in the dressing room, he said, "Our mystery guest won the Lady Byng Memorial Trophy."

Coach looked at Berk. He seemed to be choosing his words carefully. "As you all know, the Lady Byng is awarded each year to the player in the NHL who demonstrates the best sportsmanship and gentlemanly conduct."

"Sportsmanship, Berk," Ahmed said. "You probably don't know what that word means. It means being a good sport. Getting along with people."

I looked over at Ahmed. I was surprised he said that. He's usually one of the quietest guys on the team. Maybe he had had enough of Berk's behaviour, too.

Berk stared at Ahmed.

The coach continued. "Berk, a lot of times the winner of the Lady Byng Memorial Trophy doesn't have very many penalty minutes. But, besides gentlemanly conduct, he's also a top player."

"Kind of like a role model?" Aaron asked.

"Exactly," Coach answered. "And there are a few players on this team who need to work harder at good sportsmanship." He looked at Berk and Drew again.

I knew what Coach meant. I bet almost everyone did. But I wondered if Berk got the message.

After Coach left, we all tried to guess which NHL player was coming to watch our last game.

"I bet it's Sidney Crosby," James suggested.

"I think it's Alex Ovechkin," said Ozzie.

"Who do you think it'll be, Tony?" asked Matthew.

I shook my head. "I don't know," I answered. "But I can't wait to find out!"

We had just finished getting dressed for our practice when Berk called out, "Okay, Blazers!"

I knew what was going to happen next — the Bayfield Blazer chant.

The team gathered around him. All of them except me. I watched as arms were once again extended. As usual, Berk led the cheer, "Bayfield Blazers are so cool. Bayfield Blazers really rule!"

And, as usual, all the kids tapped knuckles. Except me. "Go, Blazers!" the whole team shouted. One by one, the team left the dressing room and headed out to the ice.

Chapter 15

It seemed to take forever for the last Saturday in March to come. Not only was it the final game of the season, but it was the day we got to meet a real NHL player. I was pumped.

I made sure I was at the rink extra early. I sat next to Aaron on the dressing-room bench. "So," I asked him, "who do you think it is?"

Aaron knew right away what I was talking about. "It might be Wayne Gretzky." He smiled. "I can't wait to find out!"

"Me neither."

The whole room was buzzing with excitement. And ideas.

"Michael Ryder."

"Brad Richards."

"Joe Sakic."

I finished lacing my skates. The dressing room door opened and in walked Coach. I held my breath as someone else appeared in the doorway. Who was it? He was tall and had quite a bit of grey hair and . . .

I did a double take. It was Bobby, my neighbour. What was he doing here? I peered past him, straining for a glimpse of someone else — our NHL guest. But no one else was there.

"Hey, Bobby!" I grinned.

"Hi, Tony," he answered back. "All ready for your last game of the season?"

"Yeah. We're going to win today. We'll beat the Mariners, no problem." I laughed. "So, what are you doing here? Did you come to watch the game?"

Bobby smiled at me. "Of course. Actually, your coach invited me."

I thought that was a little weird: Coach inviting two guests — Bobby and an NHL star. But maybe Coach and Bobby were good friends or something. I glanced at the door again. Still no sign of the NHL player. I didn't have any more time to think about it because Coach started to speak.

He cleared his throat. "Okay boys, listen up," he said. "Today we have a special guest visiting us." He paused and smiled at Bobby. I looked around the room. Where was the special guest? I mean, it was great that Bobby could watch me play, but right now I wanted to find out who the NHL star was. Coach began to speak again, his voice

78

interrupting my thoughts.

"I'd like to introduce our special guest — and former NHL player — Bob MacMillan." Coach turned and pointed to Bobby.

Bobby? Bobby is an NHL player? My jaw dropped. I stared at him. The neighbour who taught me how to play hockey on the pond was an NHL player? How could that be? Why didn't I know that?

Coach continued, "Bob started his NHL career before any of you were even born, back in 1974. He played with the New York Rangers and the St. Louis Blues, and he had a successful career with many other teams. But it was when he played for the Atlanta Flames in 1979 that he won the Lady Byng Memorial Trophy."

I barely heard what the coach was saying. I was vaguely aware of something about Bobby's nickname, "Mack the Knife." But all I could think was, How could I not know this? I couldn't remember him saying anything about being an NHL player. It took me a moment to realize the room had grown quiet. Coach had stopped speaking and everyone seemed to be looking at me. Even Bobby.

"Isn't that right, Tony?" he said. "I was just saying that playing the game is about attitude." He smiled. "You had such a positive attitude about learning the game. Even though you started later than most of these boys," — he swept his arm around the room — "you remained determined to be the best you could be."

I grinned back at him.

Aaron whispered, "I can't believe you didn't tell me that you knew a real NHL player."

"I didn't know it until right now," I whispered back.

"This is so cool," Aaron added.

I smiled. "Yeah."

I glanced around the room. All the kids were staring at me and I knew it was because I was friends with an NHL star.

Chapter 16

"Your coach has been telling me about all the hard work this team has been doing and the commitment you boys have to the team. I think that's wonderful." Bobby smiled as he spoke. "But your coach also asked me to talk a bit today about sportsmanship." He paused and then continued, "I guess you already know that I won the Lady Byng Memorial Trophy."

I looked around the dressing room. Heads nodded up and down.

"Well, it's important to be a team player. You've probably heard the speech about 'there is no "I" in "team"' and I'm here to remind you that that is true. Everybody on this team counts. Sure, it's fun to win. But success is about so much more than winning or losing. It's about having spirit. It's about how you play the game. Most importantly, it's about attitude. Remember, good sports are winners."

I stole a quick peek at Berk and Drew. They were both sitting really still, shoulders slumped, heads hung low.

"Now, my good friend Tony told me all about your team chant," Bobby said. "And about the knuckle tap."

Out of the corner of my eye, I saw Berk's head whip straight up. He looked over at me. His face got redder by the second.

Bobby laughed out loud. "Most teams have rituals. When I played for the Chicago Blackhawks I used to make sure that when the team headed out onto the ice, I was always third from the end of the line. Some of the guys would always eat the same meal before each game. So let's do the Bayfield Blazer ritual. Come on, guys." He signalled for the team to gather round.

Quickly the team collected in the middle of the dressing room.

Bobby looked at me. "Tony, why don't you lead the chant?"

I swallowed hard. That was something Berk always did. No one else on the team dared to do it. The Blazers had formed a circle around Bobby. Everyone was waiting for our special chant.

A terrible thought crossed my mind. What would Berk do to me if I led the chant?

I looked around for him. He was still sitting on the bench with Drew. Neither of them looked happy.

"C'mon, you two," said Coach. "You're part of the team, too."

I stood a little straighter. "Sure, I'll lead the chant," I said. "Bayfield Blazers are so cool. Bayfield Blazers really rule!"

Then everybody yelled, "Go, Blazers, go!"

We all tapped knuckles and headed out onto the ice. The last game of the season was about to begin. And I was psyched!

Chapter 17

Our last game was turning out to be a real nail-biter. It was a 3–3 tie heading into the final stretch of the third period. Matthew had faced a lot of shots on goal. I overheard Coach say to Bobby that our goalie had seen more rubber than a dead skunk on a highway. Bobby laughed. I guess that meant we were being out-shot. Badly. But we were still holding our own in the game.

Then Coach tapped my helmet. "Your line's out next, Tony. Skate hard."

The door to the players' box opened and I skated over for the faceoff. I watched Berk as he got ready for the referee to drop the puck. We were just outside the Mariners' end zone. This was our last chance to score.

"Last minute of play in the game," announced a voice on the loud speaker.

Off in the distance I could hear my mom cheering, "Let's go, Blazers!" Her cowbell rang loudly.

The puck headed my way. I skated toward the net with it. This was our chance. The Blazers could pull ahead. Berk was skating on my left. He was closer to the net than I was. Close enough that he might actually score a goal. Should I pass to him? No, he probably wouldn't be able to do it.

Then I remembered Bobby's words. *Success is about more than winning. Good sports are winners.* So I passed the puck to Berk. He closed in on the net, picking up speed. He was going to score. I could tell. It would be his first goal and we would win the game. Then he fumbled and started to wheeze.

Not now, I thought. Not when he's about to score the game winner!

"Shoot, Berk! Shoot!" I yelled.

He looked at me. I could tell he didn't have enough strength to make the shot.

"Tony!" he gasped, and his voice sounded croaky.

I watched, not really believing what I saw, but Berk passed the puck back to me. I headed straight for the net. I could see the whites of the goalie's eyes. I flipped the puck. It went sailing over the goalie's shoulder into the upper left-hand corner.

Goal!

The crowd went wild! It sounded like thunder rumbling through the rink. It was the best sound ever.

Chapter 18

After the game, the teams lined up on the blue lines. It was time for the medal ceremony.

The losing team always gets their medals first. The Malone Mariners' coach spoke a bit about his team working hard. He said he was proud of everyone's efforts. Then he hung shiny silver medals around each player's neck. I watched the players' faces as the coach presented each medal. I could tell they were happy but that they wished they had won their last game. Silver medals were good but gold ones would have been even better.

Then our coach stepped forward. First he presented everyone on the team with gold medals. Then he said, "Today we are also presenting two trophies. The winners of the trophies have been chosen by a panel of three judges. These judges are some of our most loyal fans. They have followed the progress of the Bayfield Blazers from the start of the season. But before we do the presentation, I'd like to thank them for their time and dedication." Coach clapped. We all tapped our sticks on the ice.

Coach smiled at his team. Our first award today is the Most Valuable Player Trophy. It goes to the person who kept this team in the game. He made a lot of great saves." Coach looked directly at Matthew. "Matthew, the Most Valuable Player of the Game award goes to you."

Matthew skated over and shook hands with the coach. Then Coach gave him his trophy. Matthew had the biggest smile.

"Our next trophy," said Coach, "is a new one this year. It's called the Team's Choice Award. It is an award like the Lady Byng Memorial Trophy." He looked at us. "And we all know what that trophy stands for." He glanced over at the crowd and smiled at Bob MacMillan. "This trophy goes to a player who, today, displayed the most team spirit. It is the player who put the team ahead of himself."

I looked up and down the line at our team. I wondered who the coach was talking about. It could be almost anyone. I thought about how, after Bobby's talk, everyone had worked just a little harder at playing together.

Coach continued, "This kid had a chance to score his very first goal of the season, but instead, he put the team first. Because of that, we won the game. The Team's Choice Award goes to Berk."

I looked at Berk. I could tell he was

surprised. Really surprised.
He had this look on his
face that said, Who,
me?

Slowly he skated
toward Coach. He
shook his hand.

"Good game,
Berk." Coach handed
him a gold trophy.

Berk looked at it. He ran his hands over
it. He held it high above his head. His smile
was so big that I could see he had two teeth
missing — in the exact same spot as me.

He looked at Drew and skated toward
me. I was pretty sure what that look meant.
What was he going to do? Not even Berk was
gutsy enough to push me down in front of
everybody. Or was he? Maybe he was going
to take one last chance to say something
mean. I could just hear him saying, 'Look
what I won, Tony Baloney.' I held my breath,
expecting the worst.

Then Berk made a fist. Oh no, here it comes! He's going to plow me in the face — right in front of the whole team. I squeezed my eyes shut, but I could picture Drew watching. He'd be laughing at me one more time.

Nothing happened.

I opened one eye. Berk stood in front of me, grinning.

He held out his fist at chest level and tapped the air.

Ah, I got it. I raised my fist and tapped knuckles with Berk. And we both smiled.

So that was how my first year in hockey ended. The Bayfield Blazers finished the season by winning their division. But I also got to see that there was so much more to winning than having the most points. It was about having the right attitude. It was about working together as a team. I guess maybe Berk finally understood that, too.

Chapter 19

On Monday at school, Ms MacArthur announced it was time for another round of Stump the Expert.

"This will be our last game for March," she said. "The team with the most points earns the cafeteria coupons. Tomorrow we start a new month and a brand new game. Okay, here's our first question." She reached into the basket and pulled out a slip of paper.

I crossed my fingers on both hands. I hoped it was an easy question. "Ready?" I asked Aaron and Matthew.

They both nodded. Our team was tied for first place. We had to score another point to win.

"Our first question is from the Nature category."

Behind me, I could hear Bethany whisper to Claire, "This will be easy!"

"The question is, what colour is a hippo's sweat?"

Bethany yelled out, "I know, I know!"

Ms MacArthur smiled. "Okay, Bethany, but no shouting 'I know' next time. Now, what colour is a hippo's sweat?"

"Clear," she answered.

"Sorry, that is incorrect. Does anyone else want to give it a try?"

I searched my brain, trying to remember if I ever read anything about that. "Do you guys know?" I whispered to my teammates.

"Nope," said Aaron. "I would have guessed clear, too."

"I think I might know," came a small voice from the back of the room.

I turned in my seat to see who it was. Claire. She's really smart.

"I think a hippo's sweat is red," she said.

Some of the kids in the class started to laugh.

"You're absolutely right!" said Ms MacArthur. "It's called blood sweat. That's a point for your team." She added Claire's point to the board. "Well, boys and girls, we have a three-way tie for first place."

I groaned out loud. We needed to get the next point.

"Question number two is from the Literature category," announced Ms MacArthur. "What storybook bear was named after the city of Winnipeg?"

I thought about all the books I had read about bears. *Goldilocks and the Three Bears*, The Berenstain Bears, *Corduroy*. But none of those seemed right. What bear was named after Winnipeg?

The room was quiet. I knew all the Grade Threes were trying to come up with the answer.

"Does anyone want to make a guess?" asked Ms MacArthur.

When no one answered, she said, "The bear named after Winnipeg was Winnie the Pooh."

I groaned and looked at Matthew. We should have gotten that.

"Now, for our last question today," said Ms MacArthur. "It's from the Sports category."

I sat up a little straighter. I leaned forward to make sure I'd hear the question.

"What hockey trophy is awarded to the player who demonstrates good sportsmanship and gentlemanly conduct?"

Right away my hand shot into the air. Unfortunately, so did a bunch of other hands. I looked around the room. Every Blazer had his hand up. We all knew the answer to this one. But who would the teacher pick?

"Let's see." Ms MacArthur tapped her finger against her chin. "Ozzie, you haven't answered a question in a while. Do you know the name of the trophy given for good

sportsmanship?"

Drat. I knew Ozzie would get it right. And he was on Claire's team. That meant his team would win by one point.

"It's the Lady Byng Memorial Trophy," he answered. He had a big smile on his face.

"Correct," said the teacher and she scored a point on the board.

So Claire's team won Stump the Expert. They would get the free cafeteria coupons. I thought about all the new foods that were in the cafeteria — the veggie wraps, the fruit muffins, the yogurt smoothies. My stomach growled. It sure would have been nice to try some of those things. Especially free.

I looked over at Claire's team. They were laughing and high-fiving each other. I wished it could have been me.

Then I thought of something Bobby had said when he came to visit the Blazers just before our last game. *Success is about more than winning or losing.*

"Hey, Claire!" I called out.

She looked over at me.

"Good game. Congratulations."

Claire looked surprised. "Thanks," she said. "I think I'm going to try the veggie pizza. It's got extra cheese on it." She grinned. "I hear it's pretty big. Want to try some?"

About the author

Nancy Wilcox Richards

As a kid, Nancy faithfully watched the Saturday night hockey games — with the entire family gathered in the living room to cheer on the Montreal Canadiens. On school nights during the playoffs, her dad would wake her up to watch the last minutes of the games, especially if it looked as though Montreal was going to win the Stanley Cup.

In high school Nancy played girls' hockey. She was absolutely terrible. Just like Tony, she stepped onto the ice for the first time with her skate guards on and fell flat on her face.

When her son was small, Nancy spent many cold Saturdays bundled up to her eyeballs at the rink — cheering him on and clanging a cowbell when his team scored a goal.

Nancy Wilcox Richards is the author of *How to Tame a Bully*. She teaches school in Mahone Bay, Nova Scotia.